GREAT DAY for UP

By Dr. Seuss

Pictures by Quentin Blake

A Bright & Early Book
From BEGINNER BOOKS
A Division of Random House, Inc., New York

Library of Congress Cataloging-in-Publication Data:
Seuss, Dr.   Great day for up.   (A Bright and early book, no. 19)
SUMMARY: Rhymed text and illustrations introduce the many meanings of "up."
ISBN: 0-394-82913-1 (trade) ; 0-394-92913-6 (lib. bdg.)
[1. Stories in rhyme]   I. Blake, Quentin, illus.   II. Title.   PZ8.3.G276Go   [E]   74-5517

Manufactured in the United States of America   92 91 90 89 88

UP!
UP!

The sun is getting up.

The sun gets up.

So UP with you!

UP!

Ear number one . . .

Ear number two.

Up, heads!

Up, whiskers!

Tails!

UP! UP!

Great day, today!
Great day
for

UP!

Up! Up!

You!
Open up
your eyes!

You worms!

You frogs!

You butterflies!

Up, whales!

Up, snails!

Up, rooster!

Hen!

Up!

Girls and women!

Boys and men!

Great day
for UP FEET!
Lefts and rights.

And Up! Up! Baseballs!

Footballs! Kites!

Great day
to sing
up on a wire.

UP!

Up, voices!
Louder! Higher!

Up stairs!

Up ladders!

Up on stilts!

Great
day
for up
Mt. Dill-ma-dilts.

Everybody's
doing UPs!

On bikes . . .

. . . and trees

. . . and buttercups.

Up! Up!

Waiters!

Alligators!

Up, folks!

Up in
elevators!

UP!

Up giraffes!

Great day
for seals!

Great day for UP
on ferris wheels!

UP! UP! UP!

Fill up the air.

Up, flags!
Balloons!
UP! Everywhere!

UP! UP! UP!

Great day for UP!

Wake every person,
pig and pup,
till EVERYONE
on Earth is up!

Except for me.
Please go away.
No up.
I'm sleeping in today.

Dr. Seuss

is known and loved throughout the world as the author of almost forty marvelous books for children. The most famous of all may be THE CAT IN THE HAT, a book that revolutionized reading for beginners and became the symbol of Beginner Books and Bright and Early Books.

Until now, Dr. Seuss has always drawn all the pictures for his books, but he so liked the wonderfully jolly drawings of an Englishman named

Quentin Blake

that he asked him to illustrate *Great Day for UP*. Mr. Blake, who teaches illustration at the Royal College of Art, is a very popular artist in England, where he draws for many magazines (including *Punch*) and has done several children's books. This is his first Bright and Early Book and we hope there will be many more to come.